The Little
Christmas Tree

Loek Koopmans

Floris Books

Once upon a time there was a little tree, a beautiful, healthy, green tree. But it was not happy. This little tree did not have soft, green leaves like the other trees in the forest. It had hard, sharp needles, and it did not like them.

"Why do I have such hard, sharp needles? Why don't I have soft, green leaves like the other trees?" it grumbled.

"I wish I was beautiful, the most beautiful tree in the forest. I wish I had bright, golden leaves. Yes, leaves of pure gold. That's what I'd really like!"

The little tree fell asleep and dreamed of golden leaves all night long.

The next morning when it woke up, the little tree had golden leaves. Leaves of pure gold! The little tree was delighted. It called out, "I am the prettiest tree in the forest. Just look at me!"

The little tree was happy all day long. Until night fell. And then guess what happened …

Along came a man with a big sack. "Look at that!" he said, amazed. "It's a tree with golden leaves! I'll pick them and sell them at the market. Just think how much money I'll make."

Next morning, there stood the little tree, all bare and sad.

"It's not fair! Now I have nothing," it moaned. "I want new leaves, but not gold ones. This time I want glass leaves!"

When the little tree woke up next morning, was it still bare? No, it was
covered in leaves of glass.

"Just look at me!" called the little tree. "How pretty I am with these leaves
of glass!"

When the sun shone its leaves glistened. When the wind blew gently its
leaves tinkled.

The wind started to blow stronger, until it grew into a mighty storm. The glass leaves no longer tinkled. They crashed and cracked against each other, and broke into tiny pieces.

"It's not fair!" cried the little tree. "Here I am again, all bare and sad."

"I want new leaves," it declared. "But this time I want soft, green leaves like all the other trees. Green leaves can't get broken, and you can't sell them at the market. What a good idea: lovely, soft, green leaves."

The next day when the little tree woke up, it was ever so happy because it had soft, green leaves.

"Just look at me!" called the little tree. "Now I am pretty."

And the little tree would have been happy, if only there hadn't been goats in the forest. But a goat and her kids found the soft, green leaves delicious.

There stood the little tree, all bare and sad, and stiff with fear. In a little voice it cried, "I don't want leaves any more. Not green leaves, not glass leaves, not leaves of pure gold. If only I could have my own needles back. I liked them best, after all."

Night fell, and the little tree dreamed of its own needles. When the new day dawned, the little tree laughed with joy, and all the other trees joined in, because its wish had come true. The little tree had its own needles once more.

Many weeks passed, and the little tree was content. Not just because it had its needles back, but also because winter had come and snow was falling. And that tickled!

One snowy day, the little tree heard laughter and children's voices calling out,
"Look! This must be the most beautiful tree in the forest."
  The little tree shook with joy.

And then a little shining star fell down from heaven, past all the big, tall trees, and landed snugly on top of the little tree. Now it was a real Christmas tree.

All the animals of the forest gathered around in wonder, and the mother
and her children sang merrily to the little Christmas tree.
  "This is the happiest day of my life," said the little tree.

When the mother and her children got home, they sat around a warm fire.
The mother got out a book and began to tell a story.

"Once upon a time, there was a little tree, a beautiful, healthy, green tree …"

Also by Loek Koopmans and published
by Floris Books:

Any Room for Me?
The Pancake that Ran Away
Frog, Bee and Snail Look for Snow

First published in 2008 in Dutch as *Het Boompje* by Christofoor Publishers
Text after a poem by Friedrich Rückert (1788–1866)
First published in English in 2009 by Floris Books

British Library CIP Data available

ISBN 978-086315-717-2
Printed in China